CAPTAIN
★AWESOME

VS. THE
SPOOKY, SCARY HOUSE

By STAN KIRBY

Illustrated by GEORGE O'CONNOR

LITTLE SIMON

New York   London   Toronto   Sydney   New Delhi

LITTLE SIMON

An imprint of Simon & Schuster Children's Publishing Division • 1230 Avenue of the Americas, New York, New York 10020 • Copyright © 2013 by Simon & Schuster, Inc. All rights reserved, including the right of reproduction in whole or in part in any form. LITTLE SIMON is a registered trademark of Simon & Schuster, Inc., and associated colophon is a trademark of Simon & Schuster, Inc. For information about special discounts for bulk purchases, please contact Simon & Schuster Special Sales at 1-866-506-1949 or business@simonandschuster.com. The Simon & Schuster Speakers Bureau can bring authors to your live event. For more information or to book an event contact the Simon & Schuster Speakers Bureau at 1-866-248-3049 or visit our website at www.simonspeakers.com. Designed by Laura Roode. Manufactured in the United States of America 0613 FFG

First Edition 10 9 8 7 6 5 4 3 2 1

Library of Congress Cataloging-in-Publication Data Kirby, Stan. Captain Awesome vs. the spooky, scary house / by Stan Kirby ; illustrated by George O'Connor. — 1st ed. p. cm. — (Captain Awesome ; no. 8) Summary: As Halloween nears, Captain Awesome and Nacho Cheese Man set out to protect Sunnyview from monsters but when they encounter what may be a real haunted house, they suddenly remember they have homework to do. [1. Superheroes—Fiction. 2. Halloween—Fiction. 3. Haunted houses—Fiction. 4. Schools—Fiction.] I. O'Connor, George, ill. II. Title. III. Title: Captain Awesome versus the spooky, scary house. IV. Title: Spooky, scary house. PZ7.K633529Cbs 2013 [E]—dc23 2012015173

ISBN 978-1-4424-7254-9 (pbk)

ISBN 978-1-4424-7255-6 (hc)

ISBN 978-1-4424-7256-3 (eBook)

Table of Contents

"Boo!"

Eugene McGillicudy pedaled his bike next to his best friend, Charlie Thomas Jones.

Could Halloween be any more awesome? Eugene thought.

There were the jack-o'-lanterns, the falling leaves, the chill of the autumn air. And best of all . . .

TRICK OR TREAT!

There was the dressing up in

costumes and running from house to house to collect as much candy and chocolate as your hands—or backs—could carry!

You didn't get that amount of awesomeness on Presidents' Day or even on a snow day.

And Halloween was getting closer.

Eugene and Charlie took the long way home from school. They pedaled slowly, their eyes darting from side to side. The dry fall leaves swirled across the street and crunched under the wheels of their bikes.

The town of Sunnyview went all out for Halloween. Houses were

covered in fake spider-webs and pumpkins were on every porch. One yard had a mummy in a coffin, and another had Frankenstein sitting in a rocking chair. But Eugene and Charlie weren't just enjoying the spooky scenes.

They were out on patrol.

MONSTER PATROL!

For real monsters, Halloween was like their birthday. It was a chance for them to run freely around Sunnyview without anyone thinking twice about it. In the dark no one could tell the difference between the real Count Fangula and Kieran Phillips in a vampire costume.

"You see any evil yet, Charlie?" Eugene asked.

"Just a torn paper skeleton," Charlie responded.

The boys were determined to stop Halloween evil. No monsters would ruin the greatest day in the history of free candy! Eugene and Charlie would stop them because that's what their favorite superhero, Super Dude, would do.

What's that you say?

You've never heard of Super Dude? WHAT?! Do you not have all of his comic books, movies, video games, and action figures?

Super Dude is the super superhero who once washed the evil Liquid Fury down the drain in *Super Dude and the Clean Car Wash of Cleanliness*.

Super Dude was a true hero and Eugene's favorite. He was, after all, the main reason Eugene became Sunnyview's first and most awesome superhero. Eugene was the one, the only . . . CAPTAIN AWESOME!

MI-TEE!

With his best friend, Charlie Thomas Jones (also known as the

superhero Nacho Cheese Man),
and their class pet hamster, Turbo,
Eugene formed the Sunnyview
Superhero Squad to stop the evil-
ing of bad guys.

SKID!

Eugene skidded to a stop at the edge of Mr. Muckleberry's driveway. A tingle ran up his arm and zipped through his whole body.

"What is it, Eugene?" Charlie asked. He could tell Eugene was sensing something bad.

"Shhh. Over there." Eugene pointed across the lawn. . . .

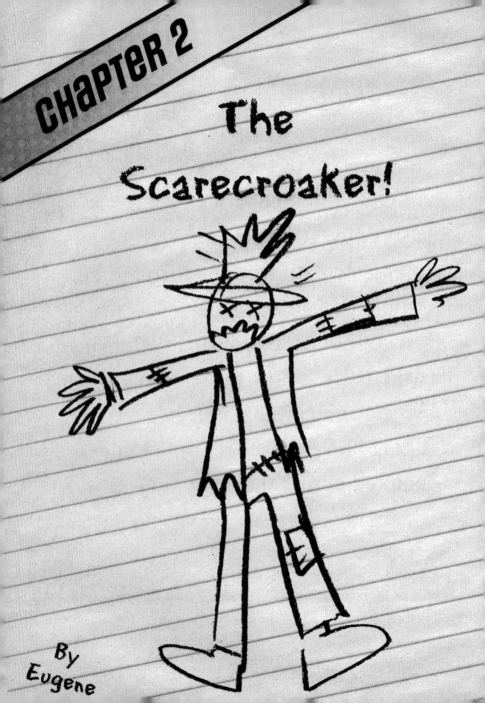

A creature stood next to Mr. Muckleberry. But not just any creature. It was the enemy of pumpkins and children everywhere: **the Scarecroaker!**

The awful scarecrow had a straw-stuffed body, floppy hat, and burlap mask covering his face. Looking like a normal scarecrow was just one of his many powers.

But Eugene knew better. The

Scarecroaker was trouble. He was just a few straws away from Mr. Muckleberry, who was working quietly in his yard hanging tiny plastic pumpkins from his maple tree.

"Mr. Muckleberry! Look out!" the boys shouted in unison.

Mr. Muckleberry didn't speak.

Oh no! He's been hypnotized by the Scarecroaker's Straw Trance! Eugene thought.

This was just like that time in the Super Dude Creepy Halloween Special No. 2, when Super Dude battled the Vampirates and their fleet of Flying Coffin Ships. He turned their wooden ships into splinters, which had, in turn, turned the Vampirates into dust.

Stopping the Scarecroaker was a job for the Sunnyview Superhero Squad!

"Hey, Scarecroaker! Stay away from Mr. Muckleberry, you evil scarecrow made of straw!" Captain Awesome jumped the MI-TEE Mobile over the curb and pedaled across Mr. Muckleberry's lawn.

"We are going to knock your stuffing into November!" Captain Awesome yelled to the Scarecroaker.

"What he said!" Nacho Cheese Man added. He pulled a can of cheese from his backpack and steered the Cheesy Rider up the driveway. "Cheesy YO!"

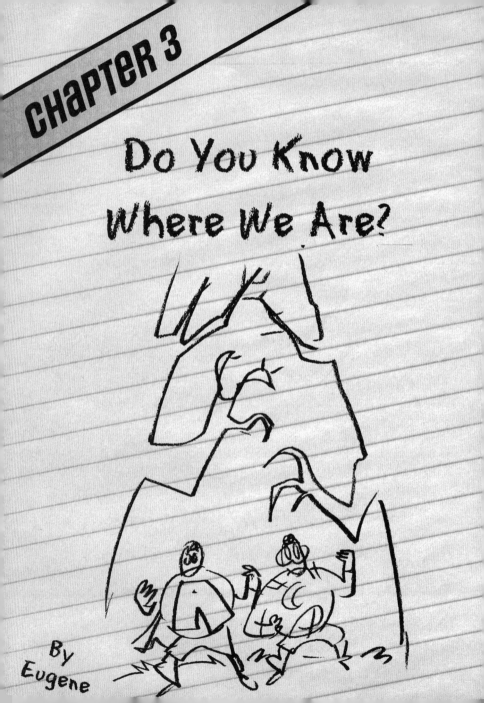

Hmmmmm. Eugene was thinking.

Hmmmmm. Eugene was thinking harder.

Hmmmmm! Ouch! He was thinking so hard his head hurt.

"Eugene?" Charlie said. "Where *are* we?"

After defeating the very evil Scarecroaker, the superheroes had sped away superfast from

Mr. Muckleberry's house. He hadn't had time to thank Captain Awesome and Nacho Cheese Man for saving his life since he was too busy raking up all the scattered straw from his lawn.

The superheroes zigged, then zagged, doubled back, turned right four times, left four times, and cut through Mr. Worth's pumpkin patch, down a dirt road, through a gravel alley, and then stopped to catch their breath.

SKID!

They ended up on the street where their friend Sally Williams lived. Her house had a glowing jack-o'-lantern on the porch and

ghosts hanging in all the windows.

"We should go say hi to Sally," Charlie suggested.

"Not now, Charlie. Look!" At the end of the street was something Eugene had never noticed before. Eugene was pointing to a yard over-grown with trees that looked like they were eating the ground under them.

FLASH!

Gasp! That was that? Eugene thought. *Is there something in the trees?*

"Charlie! My Super-Awesome Super-Vision is detecting something worth seeing. Let's go check it out."

A chill went up Charlie's spine. "Eugene! Wait! What if that's the house where the deadly Manguar, half man, half jaguar, lives? I don't think he'd want us knocking on his front door."

Too late.

MI-TEE!

Eugene jumped his bike up onto the curb and headed through the trees. Charlie sighed and pedaled to catch up.

Eugene powered through the trees that were trying to grab him and the branches that were trying to scratch him.

Charlie blasted through the jungle behind him. "Eugene! Where are you?" Charlie pushed the branches out of his way, struggling to keep his balance. "Eugene!"

Suddenly Charlie stumbled across Eugene's bike. But where

was Eugene? Charlie got off his bike and ran out of the trees. Eugene was waiting for him. A large, three-story house was in front of them.

"Look at this place, Charlie."

Sunlight gleamed off a broken attic window. The front door flopped open as if someone had punched it, shutters on the upstairs windows were crooked, and the porch railing was missing pieces. Paint was peeling so much that it looked like the house had a bad sunburn.

No one had lived there for a long time.

25

Eugene and Charlie dropped to the ground. They crept along the grass toward the front porch.

Eugene peeked over the edge. The porch was empty. "Come on, Charlie."

Charlie gulped as he followed Eugene. Keeping low to the ground, they reached the stairs.

"I think my Awesome Sense is tingling again," Eugene said.

"I think it's your Creepy Sense," Charlie said. "This house is creepy. Those windows look like eyes."

Charlie was right. Worse, the door looked like a crooked mouth laughing at them. The roof and the chimney looked like an evil top hat.

Eugene realized the horrible truth. "Charlie! This is no ordinary house at the end of an ordinary street. This house is here on purpose."

"On purpose? For people to live in, right?" Charlie asked.

"Wrong, my superhero friend! This is a house of no good!"

"I was afraid you'd say that," Charlie replied, shaking his head.

Eugene took one step forward, then paused. His whole body was tingling. He felt weird. His hands were sweaty. He looked over to where he'd left his bike. "It's getting

late. We should come back later."

Charlie started backing up across the yard.

The sun was setting. Long shadows fell across the front of the house. "You're right, Eugene. Besides, I have to get home for, uh, dinner," Charlie said. "And other kinds of stuff."

Eugene was quick to agree. "I've got to finish tonight's homework. Maybe tomorrow night's, too."

Charlie nodded. "Yep, nothing wrong with doing homework."

Eugene and Charlie ran over to their bikes and pushed them through the trees. Back on the street they hopped on the bikes and headed for home.

They made it in record time.

"Hello, house. We meet again."

That night, Eugene climbed the stairs to the porch of the abandoned house. Shadows from the overgrown trees made everything darker. And creepier.

SCRATCH!

Tree branches scraped across the windows. Eugene swallowed a lump that felt like a golf ball. He

pushed open the front door and
stepped inside the house.

CREEEEEEEEEAAKKK!

He was alone. At night. Inside the creepy old house.

Why am I here by myself? Eugene wondered.

The house was as dark as the inside of Captain Darkness's all-powerful Midnight Helmet. A breeze chilled the air and Eugene shivered.

BRRRRR.

Eugene's hand felt along the wall, trying to find a light switch. *Got it!*

CLICK!

Nothing.

CLICK-CLICK-CLICK-CLICK!

Still nothing.

Eugene smacked the wall with his hand.

WHAP!

Still no lights.

Good thing there's a full moon, Eugene thought. The moonlight shone in through the dusty, broken windows, cutting long rectangles across the wooden floor.

Eugene suddenly felt nervous. He reminded himself that superheroes may get scared, but they're still superheroes. He'd learned that from Super Dude No. 14, when Super Dude was afraid to enter Mr. Bones's Zombie Cemetery.

Super Dude went in anyway. If Super Dude could do something like that, then Eugene knew he could too. He placed his right foot onto the first step of the staircase in front of him.

CREAK!

That was the problem with old
stairs. They always creaked.

Eugene went for the
second step.

MEOW!

A black cat
jumped off the
stairs. By the time
Eugene turned to look,
the cat was gone.

Eugene shivered and climbed
the second step . . . then the third.

CREAK-CREAK!

And then he heard something
else entirely.

What was that thump? Eugene froze on the stairs like he'd been hit with a blast of Frozen Freak's Freeze Gas.

THUMP-THUMP-THUMP!

Footsteps!

THUMP-THUMP-THUMP!

The footsteps were on the second

floor. Running. And they were getting closer. Someone or some*thing*
was coming toward him.

Eugene turned to run down the
stairs. The footsteps were coming
after him. Eugene's legs felt like
rubber. His feet were like concrete
blocks. He had to get away.

TRIP!

Eugene fell down the stairs and crashed onto the floor.

OOF!

He held his breath and listened. Closer . . . closer . . . The footsteps were at the top of the stairs now. Eugene turned and saw a shadow looking down at him. He wanted to scream, but his mouth was locked tight.

"Eep" was all that came out. Eugene scrambled to his feet and ran toward the front door.

SLAM! He crashed into the door and dropped to the floor.

43

That was when Eugene woke up in his bed.

He sat up. He was shaking and sweaty. He looked around his bedroom. His Super Dude poster was on the wall. Turbo was still in his hamster cage. He was home. *A DREAM! It was all just a dream!*

No, not a dream. A nightmare!
WHEW!

"Turbo! You wouldn't believe the nightmare I had," Eugene said to the hamster.

SQUEAK-SQUEAK-SQUEAK!

Turbo was happily spinning on his wheel, unaware of the horror Eugene had just gone through.

Eugene wondered why he was nightmaring about that creepy old house. Was the house sending him a message? Or was there a new villain in Sunnyview, like the Dream Beaver or Nightmare Gnat, who was invading his sleep?

I've got to tell Charlie about this in the morning, thought Eugene.

And morning couldn't come soon enough.

"**I**'ll be a zombie!" Bernie Melnick said. "Braaaiiiinnnnsssss!"

"I'm going to be a princess!" Jessica Craven exclaimed.

"I'm going to be a *zombie* princess," said Mike Flinch. "I mean, prince. Zombie prince."

School was buzzing the next day. Halloween was getting closer, and everyone was excited about their costumes.

Evan Mason even had the perfect Halloween equation. "If I wear a pirate costume with two swords, plus two eye patches, and say 'yo ho ho trick or treat,' I'll get twice as much candy as anyone else. It's a scientific fact!"

But Eugene had something else on his mind: his nightmare. He'd been trying to tell Charlie about

it all morning, but school kept getting in the way. . . .

"Hey, Charlie!"

BRRRINNGGG! The school bell
rang.

"Hey, Charlie!"

"Please, Eugene, no talking in
class," his teacher Ms. Beasley said.

"Hey, Charlie!"

"Shhhhhh! Quiet in my library," the school librarian shushed him. Eugene recognized her right away as the twisted bookshelf mastermind, The Shusher!

By lunchtime Eugene was about to burst. He raced over to the table where Charlie was squirting blasts of Barbecue Cheese spray on the cafeteria's Surprise Nuggets.

"I've got to tell you about my nightmare. I was at the house," Eugene said. "*THE* house."

"The house that gives out the full-size candy bars and lets us go back for seconds?" Charlie asked.

"No," Eugene corrected. "The

creepy house on Sally's street!"

Charlie's mouth fell open. His eyes got wide.

Eugene continued. "I was there in my dream, I mean, my nightmare! There were footsteps and a creaky staircase! Then— *THUMP!*—someone or something came after me."

"Wow, Eugene! That's fantastic!" Charlie took a

deep breath and sucked down the last spray of canned cheese. He smiled. "I don't know how else to say it," he said. "It sounds like you got a new superpower! You can see into the future!"

"But I—"

"No buts," Charlie said. "We're going to win every game of dodge-ball! Even better: You'll know exactly when my mom's going to serve okra so I can ask to eat dinner at *your* house."

"But I don't—"

"Knowing the future is the perfect superpower!" Charlie was so excited that he was practically floating on thin air.

"Charlie, I can't see into the

future!" Eugene yelled. "I think it was just a nightmare."

Charlie slumped onto his chair. "That's too bad. Nightmares won't help me avoid okra at all."

"But there *is* something about that old house, Charlie. Something scary," Eugene said. "And we're going to find out what that is."

"We're going to find out by looking on the Internet, right, Eugene?"

Eugene's chuckle sent a chill up Charlie's spine. He knew what Eugene was thinking.

"This is a job for the Sunnyview Superhero Squad," Eugene said. "Captain Awesome and Nacho Cheese Man have to protect the citizens of Sunnyview from that creepy old house and whatever evil may be lurking inside it!"

Charlie sighed. "A superhero

has to do what a superhero has to do," he said, nodding. That was Super Dude's motto. "I'll get an extra supply of canned cheese."

"**S**oggy French fries are the best!" Jake Story cried. He grabbed a cold, limp French fry from the cafeteria food line and popped it into his mouth. He smiled and pushed the mushy mess through his front teeth with his tongue.

Usually Charlie and Eugene were more than eager to join Jake in grossing out the girls with a mushy food frenzy, but today was

different. Today was *serious*.

"We've gotta figure out how to get into that house, Charlie," Eugene said. "Any ideas?"

"Maybe we can ask our dads to go with us?" Charlie asked hopefully. "You know, as sort of a 'take your dad to superhero duty day'?"

"No way, dude!" said Eugene.

"We're trained superheroes! Our dads may be experts at barbecuing, but we don't know what's inside that house! It might have tentacles or fifty eyeballs or fifty tentacles with eyeballs!"

"F-fifty eyeballs?" Charlie looked at his cheese-covered lunch. He suddenly wasn't very hungry anymore.

"I know exactly what's in that house," Meredith Mooney said as she sat down at the last open spot at Eugene and

Charlie's table. Both boys slid away from Meredith to make room for her pigtails tied with pink ribbons. Her ribbons matched her pink shoes, pink socks, and pink dress.

"Hey! They were saving that place for me!" Sally Williams said, holding her tray of food.

Meredith stuck out her tongue and turned back to Charlie and Eugene. Sally sighed and sat at the next table.

Meredith turned back to the boys. "My older sister, Mary, went inside that house last Halloween on a double dog dare," she told them.

Meredith's claim was met with gasps from kids at several tables.

"Double dog?" Eugene let out a soft whistle.

"Now, that's one serious dare," Charlie said, shaking his head.

"Well, you don't just go into a house like that on a *normal* dare, do you?" Meredith said with a snarl. "The moon was full . . . and it was a dark, dark night! My sister opened the door and went inside, but none of the lights worked."

Just like my dream! Eugene thought.

"And then she heard it! CREAK! STOMP-STOMP! CREAK! STOMP! MOAN! GROAN!" Meredith said.

Eugene's eyes were bigger than baseballs. He sat in stunned silence. *I don't believe it! I dreamed that, too!*

Meredith continued. "My sister turned and looked . . . and she saw the headless ghost of the Sunny-view Spirit!"

"Ah! I hate ghosts!" Jake Story shouted, and ran away from the

cafeteria, leaving behind a full plate of cold fries.

No one else moved a muscle. They all stared at Meredith Mooney like they were zombies.

"The S-S-Sunnyview S-Spirit?!" Charlie stammered.

"The one and only," Meredith said spookily.

"What's the Sunnyview Spirit?" Eugene asked.

"*Oh, please!*" Meredith snapped. "Haven't you been listening? He's

the headless ghost who lives in the house! He came floating down the stairs, holding his head in his hands. Because that's what headless ghosts do. *'Grooooan!'* he groaned. *'Moaaaaaan!'* he moaned. *'Booooo!'* he booed! And then he tried to grab my sister!"

"Did she get away?" asked Sally, who was listening from the next table.

"Of course she did." Meredith rolled her eyes. "No ghost without a head is a match for *my* big sister. But the Sunnyview Spirit warned her that the next nosy kid who comes snooping around *his* house won't be so lucky. I'm sure you two are too chicken to go back there anyway."

The kids in the cafeteria looked at Charlie and Eugene, waiting for their response. Even Sally watched.

"Just because we're afraid doesn't mean we're chicken—" Eugene began.

"Yeah!" Charlie added.

"And nothing you say will make us feel bad if we *don't* go to that house—" Eugene continued.

"Yeah! Nothing you can say!" Charlie added.

"But we're still gonna go and check out this ghost story," Eugene finished.

"Yeah! We're still gonna go!" Charlie's eyes went wide. He pulled

Eugene aside. "What do you mean we're still gonna go?! Didn't you hear Meredith's story with the ghost and the head and GROAAAAAAN?"

"Did Super Dude back down when he went up against the Zombie Teachers in the School of Screams? They wanted him to do impossible math problems *and* eat brains. Even a superhero gets scared, Charlie.

But that should never stop us from doing what's good and right. And if this ghost is a bad guy, we've got to protect Sunnyview."

Charlie slumped."I hate it when you make sense."

It looked like Halloween night was going to be *extra* spooky this year.

CHAPTER 7

Beware of
the Sneaky
Sneakers!

By
Eugene

Captain Awesome and Nacho Cheese Man called an emergency meeting of the Sunnyview Superhero Squad. They sat under the school-yard slide. Today they had much more to worry about than the cafeteria's mushy food. Meredith's story about the Sunnyview Spirit made them realize they were about to face their spookiest villain yet!

"But why do we have to go on

Halloween night?" Nacho Cheese Man asked as he very nervously squirted canned cheese into his mouth. "Couldn't we go on a nice, bright Sunday morning? Maybe the Sunnyview Spirit likes to sleep in and we can catch him napping?"

"Ghosts don't sleep. And neither does the battle against bad guys and evil," Captain Awesome replied. "Halloween night is perfect. It's the one night a year we can go out after dark. . . ."

"I guess we can wear our superhero outfits as our 'costumes' so that Spirit guy never knows we're really superheroes," Nacho Cheese Man added.

"Exactly! And we'll go straight to the haunted house while the rest of the neighborhood will be

distracted by the awesome power of cavity-causing . . ."

"CANDY!" Both heroes jumped to their feet and shouted at the same time, bonking their heads on the bottom of the slide.

"I suppose we *could* go trick-or-treating to a few houses first," Captain Awesome said, rubbing his head.

"Yeah. I mean, it couldn't hurt." Nacho Cheese Man agreed faster

than he had agreed with anything else in his life. "We could always use the extra . . . um . . ."

"Energy?" Captain Awesome offered.

"Yeah! That's it. Energy!"

"So we'll trick-or-treat at a few houses *first*," Captain Awesome repeated. "Get some candy to give us some . . . *energy*. . . ."

"But let's skip Mrs. Humbert's house," Nacho Cheese Man suggested. "She only gives out toothbrushes and pennies.

Can't fight a ghost with a toothbrush and a penny. Wait a second. What *do* you use to fight a ghost?"

"Well, I guess we'll just have to read every single issue of Super Dude again to see if he has any pointers," Captain Awesome replied, eager to find any excuse he could to reread his old issues.

And so the super plan was made. Costumes! Trick-or-treating! Skipping Mrs. Humbert and her toothbrushes and pennies! Haunted house! But as Captain Awesome and Nacho Cheese Man broke out some Super Dude comics that they both just happened to keep in their backpacks for emergencies, neither one noticed a pair of high-top sneakers peeking out from a nearby tree.

Someone sneaky had been listening!

CHAPTER 8

Getting Coco-Nutty

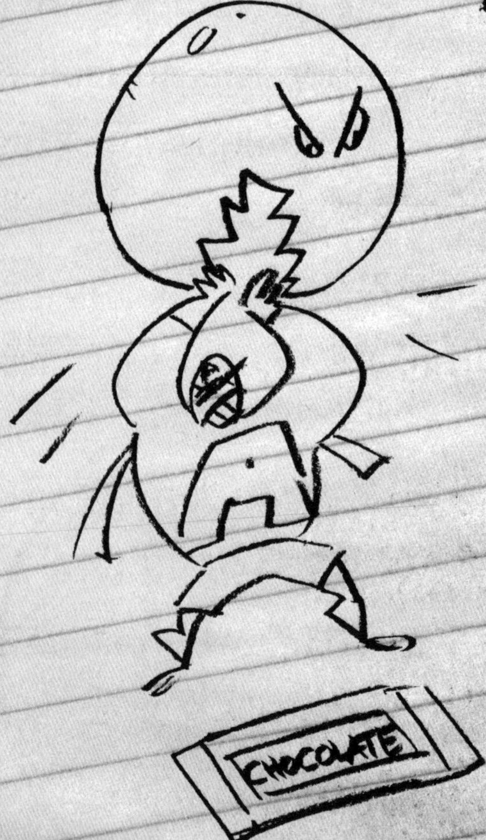

By
Eugene

HALLOWEEN!

It was every kid's dream come true and every parent's worst nightmare: free candy! And as much as you could stuff into your plastic pumpkin! There was only one goal: get enough candy to last until Easter. Oh, sure, you had Valentine's Day squeezed in there, but everyone knew Valentine's Day "candy" was just hard, sugary chalk. And Valentine's Day was the holiday of the most evil color in the world—pink!

"Safety flashlights?" Captain Awesome asked Nacho Cheese Man as the two heroes stood in front of Eugene's house going over their final checklist.

"Check."

"Safety glow sticks?"

"Check."

"Safety reflective tape?"

"Check."

"Safety parent?"
Nacho Cheese Man looked over at Captain Awesome's dad, Ned, who stood at the end of the driveway wearing a shiny gold jumpsuit, fake sideburns, and sunglasses. He kept insisting that the boys call him "Elvis."

"But just remember, Elvis, you can *only* have the candies that have coconut in them!" Captain Awesome reminded his dad.

"Ew. Coconut," Nacho Cheese Man agreed. "They only put coconut in candy so adults have something to eat."

Nacho Cheese Man was right, for he knew that all coconut candy was the creation of Coco Nut, the evil candymaker who put gross things like coconut and cherries into otherwise perfectly good chocolate, hoping to create the ultimate evil: candy that tasted terrible!

The two heroes grabbed their pillowcases, hopped onto their bikes, and rode off down the street.

At every corner, "Elvis" waited for them, not only to make sure they were safe, but to search their bags for any candy that might contain the dreaded coconut and to eat it all, saving the two heroes from the Coco Nut's coco-nutty plan.

It was a tough job, but someone had to do it.

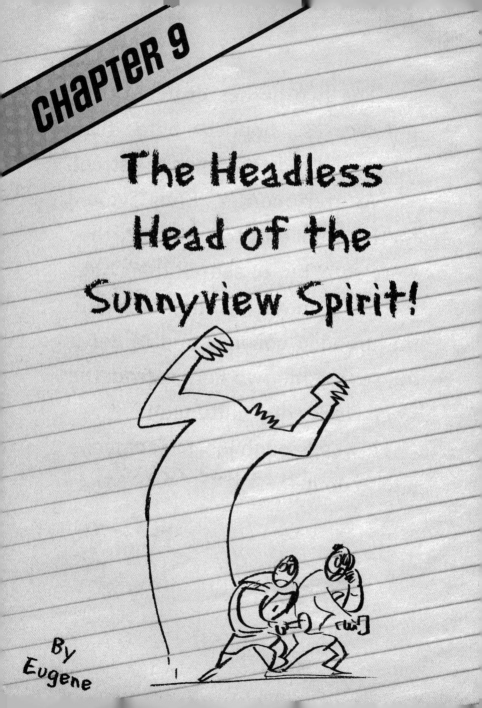

Eugene's dad stood at the corner, where parents had gathered to watch their children trick-or-treat down the street and back.

The sun disappeared behind the trees, and the street slowly began to change. The brightness of day was replaced by creeping shadows. Flashlights clicked on. Glow sticks were snapped and shaken.

Captain Awesome and Nacho

Cheese Man rode the MI-TEE Mobile and the Cheesy Rider to the spooky house at the end of the street. In the daytime it was creepy, but now, with the yard wrapped in

darkness, the house looked like it was waiting to swallow any trick-or-treater foolish enough to step onto the porch.

GULP!

The two heroes leaned their bikes against the squeaky, broken fence, took a deep breath, and dug deep into their pillowcases full of chocolately, energy-boosting candy. They each pulled out a Super Dude Super Crunch Bar full of nougatty goodness and little crunchy things. Nacho Cheese Man squirted some new pumpkin-flavored Halloween cheese onto his Super Crunch Bar, then offered the can to Captain Awesome.

"No, thanks," Captain Awesome whispered. "I don't mess with perfection."

"I'm ready when you are," said Nacho Cheese Man.

"Then let's get MI-TEE!" Captain Awesome whispered loudly. The superheroes made their way through the twisted trees and long grass toward the front door.

CREAK! CREAK! CREAK!

Each step up one of the porch stairs was met with the loud noise of old, splintered steps.

So much for sneaking up on the ghost, Captain Awesome thought.

They stopped at the top step. The only thing louder than Captain Awesome's heart pounding in his chest was Nacho Cheese Man's heart pounding in his. Captain Awesome took a step onto the porch.

MEOW!
SCREAM!
RUN!

The two heroes bolted down the steps and tumbled into a heap at the horrible sound of . . . a *cat*?

"Hey! That's Mr. Whiskersworth!" Captain Awesome whispered. "Sally's cat! What's he doing *here*?"

Mr. Whiskersworth scampered onto the porch and sat, licking his paws.

Captain Awesome jumped to his feet. "He's here to lead the charge! Come on! Let's go!" CHAAARRRGE!" Nacho Cheese Man shouted, wildly squirting

the pumpkin-flavored Halloween cheese all over the place.

"MI-TEEEEEEEEEEE!" Captain Awesome yelled while trying to avoid being hit by wildly squirted pumpkin-flavored Halloween cheese. "By the authority of the Sunnyview Superhero Squad, we command you to show your headless head, Sunnyview Spirit!"

CREAK!

Captain Awesome's eyes went wide. It was just like in his dream.

GROAN!

And then, from around the corner of the house, came something
that was not a cat! It raised its arms
above its head. In the light of the
full moon, Captain Awesome and
Nacho Cheese Man could see that
it was . . .

A GHOST!
THE SUNNYVIEW SPIRIT!

CHAPTER 10

The Rotten Plan of Princess Pinky from Ponytopia!

By
Eugene

"**O**oooooooh!" the Sunnyview Spirit groaned.

Captain Awesome and Nacho Cheese Man were stunned. They stood on the porch like two cos-tumed statues as the Sunnyview Spirit crept closer.

STOMP!
STOMP!
STOMP!

Suddenly something jumped

between Captain Awesome, Nacho Cheese Man, and the Sunnyview Spirit! It was hard to tell in the moonlight, but it looked to be the same superhero who had saved Eugene's spelling bee trophy!

"Hold it right there!" the mystery hero said to the Sunnyview Spirit, her sneakers glowing bravely in the moonlight.

"Aaaah!" the ghost shouted, and fell backward.

Aaaah? Captain Awesome thought. *What kind of a ghost says "Aaaah!"?*

And then Captain Awesome saw something that made him gasp. The Sunnyview Spirit was wearing pink slippers!

"There's only one person *I* know who'd wear pink slippers on

Halloween . . . or ever!" Captain Awesome said as he reached down and yanked a white sheet off of the supposed Sunnyview Spirit.

"*Meredith Mooney?*" Nacho Cheese Man and the mystery hero said, gasping.

"Get your hands off me, you stinky stinkers!" Meredith shouted.

She jumped to her feet and adjusted her pink princess dress.

Then she pulled out a pink plastic tiara and angrily put it on her head. "You made me bend my tiara!"

"What are *you* doing here, Meredith?" Captain Awesome asked. "Or should I say . . . Little Miss Stinky Pinky?!"

"I'll have you know that *I* am Princess Pinky from the Planet

Ponytopia," Meredith announced, turning up her nose.

"More like Princess Pukey from the Planet *Grosstopia*,"Nacho Cheese Man replied.

"When I heard you in the cafeteria talking about coming to the house, I decided to scare you guys by dressing up as a ghost,"Meredith proudly confessed.

"But what about the Sunnyview Spirit?" Captain Awesome asked.

"I made that up. My sister never got past the fence. She was too scared," Meredith explained. "But you guys can't tell my mom!" she whined. "Please, please, please!"

"I don't know. . . . ," Captain Awesome said. "Trying to scare us was pretty rotten. I think your mom might want to know what you did."

"I'll give you all my candy!" Meredith pleaded.

"DEAL!" all three superheroes replied at once.

"You're free to go, Miss Stinky Pinky," Captain Awesome began, "but you must promise to be good and never—"

"Yeah, fine, be good, whatever, I promise," Meredith said as she ran

from the house. She paused briefly at the broken fence to stick her tongue out one last time at Captain Awesome, Nacho Cheese Man, and the mystery hero.

CHAPTER 11

The Mystery Hero Mystery . . . Solved!

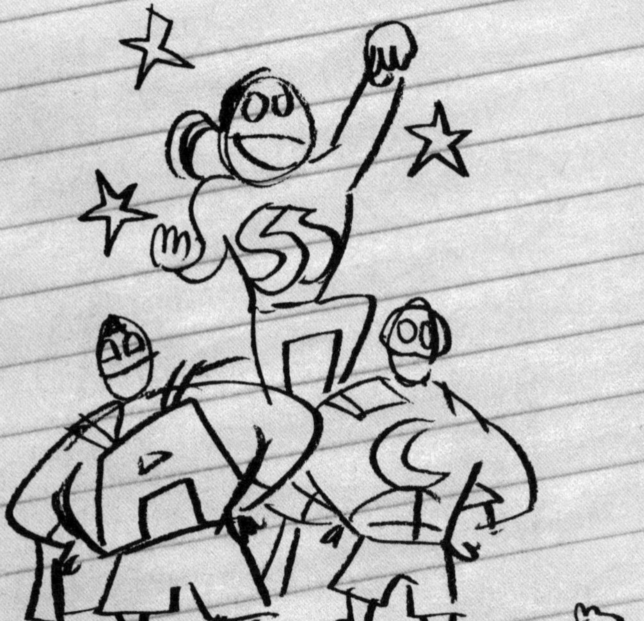

By Eugene

"**H**ow did you know we'd be here?" Captain Awesome asked the mystery hero.

"I heard you guys making your plans," she said. "Thought it might be a good idea to come in case you needed backup. But I better go—"

"Wait!" Captain Awesome said, stopping her. "This is the second time you've helped us, and we don't even know your name!"

"You can call me Supersonic Sal. This is my sidekick, Funny Cat."

Nacho Cheese Man elbowed Captain Awesome. "Ask her," Nacho Cheese Man whispered.

"No, *you* ask her," Captain Awesome whispered back.

"No, *you!*"

"Ask me what?" Supersonic Sal said.

"Well, since you've proven yourself to be a skilled superhero *twice*, we'd like to know if you want to join the Sunnyview Superhero Squad," said Captain Awesome.

"Yeah! We do all kinds of cool stuff like go on patrol, fight evil, and eat lots of brownies!" Nacho Cheese Man added.

"Sure," Supersonic Sal said coolly. "I'll catch you guys later!"

Sal headed for

the front gate, where her bike was. Funny Cat scampered after her.

"Hey! What's your real name?" Captain Awesome called out, but Supersonic Sal didn't reply. She just rode down the street in a flash.

"I guess we'll never know her real name. . . . ,"Nacho Cheese Man said, sighing.

"Or will we?"Captain Awesome said with a grin as Supersonic Sal rode her bike up the driveway to Sally Williams's house and raced inside. Both boys couldn't help but laugh. All this time the mystery hero had been Sally!

"I don't even think Super Dude could've figured that one out!" Nacho Cheese Man said.

The superheroes walked over to their bikes. They looked back

at the old house before they left. It was still the same house that had haunted Eugene's nightmare, but now that they had faced their fears, it just didn't seem so spooky anymore. Captain Awesome reached into his pillowcase and pulled out two Super Dude Super Crunch Bars. He handed one bar to Nacho Cheese Man.

Evil had been defeated, and there was still time to stock up on candy. Captain Awesome knew there was only word for a moment like this:

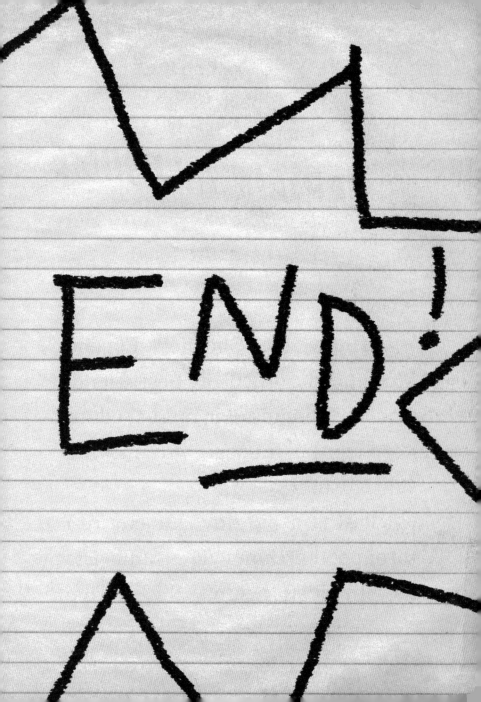

Keep reading for a sneak peek at the next Captain Awesome adventure!

CAPTAIN AWESOME
GETS CRUSHED

RUN!

"Hurry up, Charlie!" Eugene McGillicudy urged his best friend. Charlie Thomas Jones rushed to keep up, but Eugene was moving superfast.

It was a big day! Eugene ran through the Sunnyview Mall. His feet thudded against the marble floor. His heart raced. He could smell the new comic books like a dog smells bacon.

YUM!

This was all because today was **New Comic Book Day!**

I love the sound of that, Eugene thought. Then he thought it again.

New Comic Book Day!

It was the greatest day ever for Eugene, Charlie, and all comic book fans—the day when all the new comic books for the week came out. It was like Christmas, wrapped up in a birthday, in a bucket of Halloween candy.